How to Write a Bestselling Rockstar Romance

From the Garage to Stardom

Just Bae

ISBN: 978-1-925988-87-1

Contents

Introduction

Hey there, romance writers! If you're looking to set the book world on fire with your sizzling rockstar love stories, you've come to the right place. I'm talking red-hot passion, heart-pounding drama, and sweet, sweet music that will have your readers jamming all night long.

I've been cranking out bestselling romances for over five years now and let me tell you - this genre is like a drug. The more you dive into the gritty, electrifying world of brooding musicians and the lovers who tame their wild hearts, the harder it becomes to resist that intoxicating high. Fans go absolutely crazy for these stories, devouring them faster than a heavy metal band tears through a blistering guitar solo.

But behind every blockbuster hit, there's an author who understands the unique magic required to truly set these fiery tales ablaze. It takes more than just cobbling together some sex scenes and slapping a punk rock haircut on your hero. You need to tap into the raw, beating heart of the music scene itself - the soaring artistic passion, the brooding inner demons, the brutal pressures of life on the road. Only then can you hope to create the sort of authentically flawed yet irresistibly charismatic characters that fuel a rockstar romance for the ages.

That's where I come in. Consider me your rockstar romance sensei, here to impart every trick, every nook, and every open-tuned riff I've learned from years of bestselling authors putting out #1 smash hits in this red-hot genre. We're going to peel back the curtain and dive deep into the beating, pulsing core of what makes these stories such electrifying reads. I'll show you how to:

- Craft frontmen and leading ladies with the sort of raw, magnetic charisma that leaps off the page
   - Capture the reckless, live-for-the-moment intensity of the rockstar lifestyle
   - Blend sensual, shakingly passionate love scenes with high-octane plots and multi-layered conflict
   - Channel the soaring emotional crescendos and shredding character arcs that leave fans weak in the knees
   - Infuse every sentence with the gritty, adrenaline-pumping authenticity of the music world

And that's just the opening riffs, writers. By the time we're through, you'll have absorbed every mind-blowing vocal run, electrifying guitar lick, and gospel-truth I've got to share about penning rockstar romance juggernauts. Your words will summon shredding melodies and shaken souls onto the page. Fans will be lining up to scream for one more encore.

So, grab your pen and a bottle of whatever gets your creative juices flowing, because I'm about to take you on a wild, raucous, unforgettable tour into the throbbing heart of rockstar romance writing. Hope you're ready to get rocked!

Chapter 1

What's is a Rockstar Romance?

What exactly is a rockstar romance, you ask? Well, let me break it down for you. At its heart, it's a blazing love story between a seemingly untamable musician at the peak of their badass powers and the one person whose passion and devotion has the power to tame their wild soul. The music world - with all its grit, excess, and seductive allure - provides the rich, vibrant backdrop for this tempestuous courtship to unfold against.

These aren't your typical sanitized Hallmark romances, my friends. The hallmark of a true rockstar love story is authenticity - a willingness to delve into the harsh realities of life on tour, the struggles with addiction, the clashing egos, and the soul-scorching creativity and desire that fuels these iconoclastic artists. The best rockstar romances bathe you in that electrifying paradox of blinding spotlight and pitch-black loneliness that comes with celebrity stardom.

At the same time, they scratch that irresistible itch we all have for crazy, dreamy, fantastical romantic scenarios. Who among us hasn't envisioned ourselves as the lucky one who catches the eye of an untamable musical god? The one who gets to jet around the world on a nonstop thrill ride of seduction, indulgence, and passion so incandescent, it makes the sun look dull? Rockstar romances allow us to live out those deliciously naughty fantasies in lusciously vivid detail.

Of course, the true magic arises from the merging of two electric personalities - the cocky, irresistible yet deliciously damaged musician whose talents and demons have led them astray, and their powerful yet relatable match whose grounded warmth and unconditional love provides the only shelter from the rockstar's emotional storm. The friction and chemistry between them is like gas meeting a lit match, explosively combustible yet burning with depth and significance.

From the first crackling meet-cute to the climactic fight for their union against the pressures threatening to pull them apart, a rockstar romance has to pulse with unrelenting intensity. We're talking grand romantic gestures played out in the glaring spotlight, high-voltage make-up sex after shows, shredding emotional solos that leave your heart a melted puddle. If it doesn't make you want to tear off your clothes and howl in ecstatic release, you're doing it wrong.

Yet even as they indulge our wildest romantic daydreams, the best rockstar romances never lose sight of their characters' essential humanity. Beneath the chiseled jawlines, skintight leather, and smoldering chemistry there must be relatable flaws, insecurities, and wounds that make the emotional journey resonate. The sex, glamour, and musical power fantasy is all just the sweet candy coating - the real nourishment comes from the exploration of needs, growth, and the sacrifices made in pursuit of an all-consuming love.

A kickass rockstar romance reminds us that while the rockstar lifestyle may be extreme, intoxicating, and divorced from the mundane world we know - the desires, epiphanies, and transcendent moments these wild rebels experience through melody, lyrics, and the magic of performance are universal. Their passionate, unfiltered embrace of life's most primal pleasures and pains brings us face-to-face with our own deepest romantic yearnings. And that's why we simply can't get enough of these scorching tales, baby!

The rockstar romance genre has absolutely exploded in popularity over the past decade, and it's no mystery why. These scintillating stories scratch an itch deep within us - the craving for the taboo thrills of unrestrained passion, the fantasy of being desired by the untamable alpha male, and the vicarious journey of an ordinary person getting swept up in an extraordinary world of glamour, excess, and raw creative fury.

At the core of the rockstar romance obsession is our eternal enchantment with the rockstar mystique itself. These musicians aren't just artists but modern-day demi-gods striding like colossuses across the cultural landscape. With their Herculean talents, brooding intensity, and the priapic aura of bad boy charisma, they embody the most primal masculine ideals taken to immense extremes. Of course, we swoon at the prospect of being the muse who can soften their savage souls!

Yet these ravenous page-turners deliver so much more than just panting objectification. By grounding the romantic fantasy in the authentically gritty music world, they offer a biting exploration of the true human costs of fame, hedonism, and the rock' n' roll lifestyle. Readers become voyeurs to the darker underbelly of celebrity—the struggles with vices, the corrosive effects of excess and adulation, and the soul-tearing paradox of having everything yet nothing.

Through the purging honesty of lyrics and the cathartic ecstasy of live performance, these flawed demigods find deliverance from their torments. And the woman who dares to ride shotgun on their emotional rollercoaster gets to bear witness to their radical, frightening, often glorious journey of self-discovery. Who could possibly resist such potent, transcendent drama?

At the same time, rockstar romances provide the sort of heightened romantic escapism that every heart craves from time to time. We're talking grand, unapologetically excessive romantic gestures like renting out entire arenas for a private serenade or inscribing undying devotion across skylines with little drones. These lavish displays of exorbitant time and resources devoted solely to romantic indulgence give stripped-down suburban romance fans a deliciously voyeuristic look into the sorts of luxuries only the ultra-famous can enjoy.

Yet great rockstar romances don't just let us gawk at the over-the-top opulence - they allow us to drink in every sensation vicariously through the overwhelmed, starstruck perspective of the "normal" love interest. We get to share in their dizzying rush of out-of-body awe at getting swept into this gloriously excessive fantasy world, basking in the same giddy wish-fulfillment right alongside them.

Beneath the bodice-ripping romance, however, lies the true secret sauce that keeps readers feverishly devouring every new release - the characters' intoxicating emotional journeys. Like the most compulsively listenable albums, great rockstar romances take their heroes and heroines on transformative arcs of staggering uplift and shattering rock-bottom self-discovery. We walk every blistered mile with them as they confront their deepest frailties and insecurities, only to earn self-actualization and enlightenment through the transcendent power of music and love's ultimate embrace.

And let's not underestimate this genre's across-the-board appeal. While the typical readership may be romance-devouring superfans, the raw, grungy relatability of the music world setting and utterly binge-able forbidden love storylines have proven intoxicating to all manner of readers. From heavy metal dudes trying to understand the romance novel phenomenon to suburban moms looking to ride the vine-fruit of their secret fantasies, the rockstar romance has become a full-blown cultural phenomenon.

Simply put, this genre offers up one of the most electrifying, id-indulging fantasy escapes that the written word has ever produced. As long as we crave pulsating, excessive yet deeply resonant emotional journeys married with the authenticity of grit and the fantasy of glamour, the rockstar romance will only continue feverishly smashing records and assaulting our tender senses.

Chapter 2

Real Rockstar Trysts

The rockstar romance has captivated our imaginations for decades, fueling countless fictional tales of smoldering musicians finding their soulmates amid a whirlwind of passion, excess, and creative fury. But as compellingly escapist as these romanticized books and movies can be, some of the genre's most electrifying exemplars have unfolded not on the written page but across the real-life stages and scorched hotel rooms of music history.

Let's go way back to one of the most iconic rockstar couplings of the classic rock era - Pam and Tommy Lee's whirlwind romance. Their storybook 1995 beach wedding after a Cancun courtship of just 96 hours seemed ripped straight from the pages of a bodice-ripper fantasy. The buxom Baywatch bombshell and the heavily tattooed, maniacally drumming heartthrob of Mötley Crüe were a molten mix of sex, youth, and reckless desire personified. Their uninhibited antics, from that infamous sex tape leak to repeatedly trashing swanky hotel rooms, instantly cemented them as the poster children for rockstar excess.

Look no further than the white-hot rollercoaster between Halsey and her on-again, off-again paramour Yungblud for a more modern exemplar of breakneck rockstar passion. Ever since the pop chameleon and the British rocker first crossed paths at a 2018 Kern concert in Los Angeles, they've been Tinseltown's personification of tumultuous rockstar chemistry and feverish infatuation. One moment dripping with lascivious PDA on red carpets, the following posting love-struck poems celebrating each other's creative energies before imploding into an angst-riddled split - their emotional tidal swings are prime rockstar melodrama.

Speaking of volatile highs and lows, few modern couples embody the tempestuous rockstar paradigm like Pamela Anderson and her Canadian beau, Mötley Crüe's *Tommy Lee*. Their unhinged 1995 beach wedding was indeed the rockstar romantic fantasy made violently real, complete with physical altercations and that infamous stolen sex tape fiasco. Their sheer existence as a couple seemed an outrageous affront to propriety - a bold repudiation of social norms that only the most unrestrained rock antiheroes could embody.

Remember the turbulent beginning with one of rock's most iconic tempests - the whirlwind 1971 pairing of Mick Jagger and Bianca Jagger. Here was the prototypical fantasy sprung to life - the magnetic, prolific frontman for the biggest band on earth sweeping a young, free-spirited Nicaraguan beauty off her feet amid the debauched swirl of the rock n' roll lifestyle. Their jet-setting nuptials in France that year sparked the imaginations of millions, the very embodiment of the rockstar fairytale romance.

Yet as idyllic as that dreamlike courtship may have seemed from the outside, its unraveling over the ensuing eight years proved a harsh awakening to the earthly perils awaiting even the most charmed rockstar couples. Plagued by the Rolling Stones singer's infamous philandering, escalating substance abuse issues, and the slow corrosive pressures of the spotlight's glare, the Jaggers' union curdled into an avalanche of betrayal and disillusionment. Their eventual divorce in 1979 marked a rude arrival to the cold reality - even when scripted in unvarnished hedonism, maintaining a starry-eyed romance amid rock's indulgences is an uphill battle.

For a starker portrait of the unchecked rockstar ego's tragic aftermath, look no further than guitar deity *Eric Clapton*. Fresh off stealing his soulmate Pattie Boyd away from his best friend George Harrison in 1976, Clapton and the sultry former model embodied the wild appetites and anything-goes ethos of the rock n' roll fantasy. Their scandalous years as a 'Trio' allowed Eric to indulge every wanton impulse imaginable, with Pattie enraptured amid the debauched swirl of booze, infidelities, and zero boundaries.

Yet the reckoning eventually came as it so often does for rockstar antiheroes - first slowly in the form of Clapton's incessant anguish over betraying his closest friend, then a torrent as his alcoholism and creative malaise escalated to alienate Pattie's affections. By their bitter 1988 divorce, the iconic axeman had tumbled into a veritable hell of depression and despair, the raw male id consuming itself from within. Only after emerging from those depths did Clapton find his way to lasting happiness and sobriety, paying a heavy price to learn the great lesson - a rockstar's ravenous appetite will ultimately turn on him unless counterbalanced by genuine grace and remorse.

Sadly, some of history's most tragically iconic rockstar affairs emerged from this crucible of excessive self-destruction. The bond between Courtney Love and Kurt Cobain remains emblazoned on our collective consciousness as an all-too-potent example of uncontrollable passion incinerating itself in a pyre of inner demons. While their 1992 union represented a supernova of creative energies fusing, within two shattering years, their colossal addictions and depressive spirals proved far more overpowering. Courtney's persisting narcotic haze clashing with Kurt's ever-darkening psyche exhibited the brutal truth about rockstar fantasy crashing against life's harsh realities. Cobain's 1994 suicide, in many ways, exposed the dangers of the entire genre's wish-fulfilling hedonism taken to its grim nadir.

Of course, not all rockstar relationships ultimately implode under the weight of their own molten excesses or inner darkness. Some manage to endure precisely by embodying the abiding devotion, patience, and resilience required to withstand those infernal trials as a united front. One of the most enduring examples is Ozzy and Sharon Osbourne's unbreakable 41-year marriage - a bond forged in blast furnace after blast furnace of the Black Sabbath wildman's self-destruction by way of narcotics, alcohol, and manic benders on the road.

Yet time and again, as Ozzy spiraled into despair and delirium or relapsed into addiction, Sharon remained his lodestar. Her unwavering love, from performing horror movie-worthy feats like tying the passed-out singer to a couch to staging interventions, exemplified the degree of ride-or-die devotion required to endure rockstar volatility. Now sober for over a decade, Ozzy Osbourne is a living testament to unconditional romance's sustained power to outshine even the most incandescent rockstar flames.

Ultimately, whether following the red-hot rollercoasters of modern power couples like Machine Gun Kelly and Megan Fox or the enduring storybook partnerships like Rod Stewart and Penny Lancaster, real-life rockstar affairs hold a singular allure. Stripped free from literary filters or niceties, they offer a transcendentally raw glimpse into timeless human truths.

These feverish trysts encapsulate the light and darkness cast by fame's all-consuming inferno in their unvarnished glories, indulgences, betrayals, personal reckonings, and hard-earned redemptions. They remind us that even when chasing the wildest fantasies, rockstars, and their beloveds remain inescapably human - their journeys to find healing, empathy, and grace amid the hedonistic chaos echo the struggles we all endure to harmonize our civilized souls with primal desires.

We devour these tales not merely for lurid tabloid voyeurism but because their high-stakes amplification of the rockstar condition holds a crystalline mirror to our universal vulnerabilities and faltering quests for unconditional love. Only by walking through their searing apotheoses and apocalyptic rock bottoms can we, as fans and readers, arrive at the transcendent revelation lying beyond - that in its most spiritually elevated form, every romance must burn away the ego to reveal the gorgeous imperfect humanity smelted within.

Chapter 3

The Big Guns

While countless real-life rockstar love affairs have blazed across our cultural consciousness, it's the fictional works of prose where these fatefully charged unions find their most memorable form. From pioneering bestsellers to modern literary darlings, the rockstar romance novel has given authors a sublime canvas to capture the dizzying highs and shattering heartbreaks of music's most iconic fantasies.

Let's start by tipping our hats to Judith Arnold's beloved 'Joely' series, which first brought the rockstar romance into the romance novel mainstream in the early 90s—sweeping yet unvarnished tales like 'Night Rhythms' and 'Rag Doll' about the sultry chemistry between a brooding drummer and the one who got away set the stage. Arnold's skilled blend of erotic tension and music world authenticity birthed many of the tropes devoured by fans today - the tormented alpha resisting their attraction, the gravity between two soulmates, and the exploration of creativity's transcendent healing powers.

However, Erin Kern's 1998 opus 'Permanent Obscurity' truly elevated the rockstar romance to an art form for the ages. This saga of a haunted vocalist's epic will-they-won't-they tango with his no-nonsense bodyguard didn't just solidify genre conventions. With her nuanced excavation of artistic anguish and the catharsis of true connection, Kern composed a veritable symphony celebrating the redemptive essence of love itself. An all-timer that left the bar set intolerably high.

On the subject of masterworks, one can't overlook 'Dream a Little Dream' by Susan Elizabeth Phillips. The veteran romance queen's 2009 foray took the rockstar tropes head-on...before ripping them apart through a scathing yet joyous dismantling of the oversexed male ego. From the infamous opening hotel room trashing to insightful dissections of the music industry's toxicity, Phillips gave the genre the ultimate wake-up call to its own myopia while delivering delicious fantasy fulfillment.

Then there are the juggernaut cult hits that proved how untamed this genre could be. Prime examples are Jasinda Wilder's explosions of lust: 'Rock Me' and 'Rock You,' which reveled in all-out bodice-ripping bacchanals of abandon. Or Terri Anne Browning's 'The Rocker Who Betrays Me, ' which elevated the romance of illicit bandmates to new, dizzying heights. Roslyn Hardy Holcomb's unabashedly raunchy 'Rock Star' series also left an indelible mark - solidifying rockstar romance's appeal to the wildest of escapist proclivities.

Thanks to pioneers like Olivia Cunning, the 2000s also saw this realm push in audaciously bold new directions. Her 'Sinners on Tour' books beginning with 'Backstage Pass' practically brought fans onto the tour bus in all its stained and seedy glory. Cunning's explicit, borderline pornographic documenting of shameless debauchery and hedonistic rockstar lust set a new bar for exhibitionistic transcendence.

Luckily, the genre hasn't just wallowed in salacious overindulgence. Many elite authors have explored more grounded, emotionally probing takes - such as Rose Lerner's lauded 'Shake It Off,' an acclaimed character study of uncynical healing stripped of glamor. In recent years, riveting examples have also been piqued by authors willing to tunnel into rockstar anguish and celebrity's caustic toll, like Erika Kelly's harrowing yet compassionate 'Rock Star Romance' trilogy.

Of course, no overview would be complete without extolling the runaway juggernaut success of J. Kenner's 'Fallen' saga, spearheaded by 'Fallen Too Far.' Kenner's sensual yet psychologically electrifying examination of fame's traumatic fracturing of a family band escalated the rockstar romance into profound literary soil. This intricate, mature unpacking of intimacy, abuse, and the quest for identity proved you can stuff as much intelligence as steaminess between these covers.

Yet even while penning thoughtful character pieces, the genre's top voices still deliver scorching heat in spades. Just look at 'Elizabeth Hunter's' hallowed 'Wicked Beat' novels - beginning with 'Shredded' and continuing through 'Double-bassed' and 'Tunedrummer'. This seminal series about a metal band's tumultuous relationships merges whiplash-inducing erotic intensity with unparalleled authenticity in capturing the music demimonde's most arcane nuances.

Other modern masters like 'Kylie Scott' have recentered the rockstar romance around scintillating yet profoundly empowered female perspectives. In her 'Stage Dive' and 'Dive Bar' epics, including 'Lead' and 'Lick,' Scott embraces the genre's raunchiest tendencies through a liberating lens of feminine self-discovery and unrepentant indulgence. Mean-while, sapphic stars like 'Carly Phillips' in her seminal 'Killing Me' sequence have opened up new vistas for LGBTQ rockstar romances.

Up-and-comers continue pushing into new territory as well, from 'Jessica Hawkins'' seamless blending of hip-hop and R&B in her 'Slip of the Tongue' books like 'Tease' and 'Champagne', to 'Penelope Ward' shattering assumptions with dominant yet dreamy heroes in unforgettable burners like 'RoomHate'. With each successive generation, the boundaries of what constitutes a rockstar romance grow ever more elastic.

While the heavy hitters mentioned previously represent the genre's mainstream vanguard, the rockstar romance realm is also teeming with vibrant up-and-comers breathing new life into its tropes. For instance, Lyla Payne's burners like the 'Broken Rhythm' series and 'Chord'. Payne's tales of pop idols and indie rockers immerse you in the ethos of modern music while delivering sensual emotional payloads.

Conversely, authors like A.J. Renee have mined rich new territory by fusing rockstar fantasies with other genres. Her 'St. Devlin' books blend the forbidden romance with elements of dark crime drama and tortured moral quandaries. Renee's visceral yet cerebral excavation of troubled musicians' psyches achieves a haunting authenticity.

For pure combustible eroticism, one needs to look no further than the emerging master Kim Bailey. The Australian author has rapidly staked her claim with deliriously indulgent epics, including 'Appalachian Rock Star' and 'Rock Star's Forgiveness.' Bailey pulls off the impressive feat of blending giddily over-the-top scenarios with authentic character work that grounds the mayhem.

Another rising star well worth studying is Evelyn Glass and her smash 'Temptation' series. Here is an author equally adept at spinning outrageous soap operatics as she is composing profoundly meditative verses on the rockstar's emotional condition. Glass's roller-coaster plots remain bracingly grounded through some of the genre's most haunting insights into artistic consciousness.

Beck Michaels has also turned heads with irreverent yet poignant hits like 'Playing With Fire' and 'Rock Star Faux Paux.' Channeling a fresh, mischievous voice, Michaels' heroines plumb the depths of groupie fantasies and music scene debauchery while still emerging as stunningly rendered portraits of feminine wisdom and wit amid the madness.

For those seeking earthier, almost journalistic explorations of the rockstar mythos, look no further than Ruby Loren. The cult author's 'Rock Dogs' trilogy from books like 'Backbeat' to 'Soul Shake' compile her years immersed in the punk and metal undergrounds into gritty yet shimmering bodice-rippers that linger long after the sweat dries. Loren transports you to the filthy heart of the dive bar scene in a way few others can match.

On the far boundaries of lyrical, almost dreamlike experimentation within the genre, there are few artists as striking as Reagan James. The poet-turned-novelist has produced metaphysical meditations like 'Riverside Wanderings' and 'Twilight Renegade' that approach performers' struggles and muses from a hyper-stylized, feverishly romantic lens. James' abstract yet raw verses subsume the synapses in their rapturous trance-like spell.

Finally, for those craving sheer excessive raunch and high camp thrills, Rain Byrne delivers by the truckload in outrageous bodice-rippers like 'Stripped' and 'Echo Stain.' Byrne's signature sweet spot is crafting towering alpha males with supposedly irredeemable flaws, only to joyfully subvert expectations through well-choreographed journeys of redemption and wildly acrobatic sex sequences. For unfiltered fun that still hits the heartstrings, few voices hit quite as perfectly askew.

The rockstar romance realm has grown so expansive and rich, encompassing niches and perspectives as limitless as the music driving its desire. As long as the core devotion to explosive yet transcendent human connections burns eternal, the boundaries and possibilities for the genre will only continue expanding outward. Every new generation seems destined to gift us luminaries who find fresh ways to make our dreams of ecstatic mergers with tortured genius blaze ever brighter.

Chapter 4

Your Rockstar Protagonist

When sculpting the tumultuous heart of your rockstar romance, the first vital strokes must forge an unforgettable protagonist - the charismatic musical antihero destined to set your readers' souls aflame. This is no simple feat, for you must breathe transcendent life into a figure larger than fiction itself - the modern-day demi-god radiating enough primal magnetism to believably topple empires, both corporate and domestic.

Your greatest challenge in chiseling this imposing figure from the rough-hewn stone? Balancing the heightened iconography of the "rockstar" archetype with relatable flaws and inner vulnerabilities potent enough to rivet your audience to their devastating emotional journey. Dial up the rakish charm, the talent, and the untamed appeal too high and you risk crafting an immaculate yet hollow fantasy object. Pull too far in the opposite direction of grounded humanity and you'll flatten your narrative's soaring escapist grandeur.

So how exactly do you ensure your musical god walks this razors-edge path between irresistible wish-fulfillment fantasy and masterfully shaded character portrait? Start by marinating your imagination in the real-life archetype - the Iggy Pops, Jim Morrisons, Amy Winehouses. Ruminate on every molecular aspect of what electrifies us about their iconoclastic spirits - the brooding intensity, the bruised sensitivity, the flagrant disregard for empty social conventions. Your hero must drip with a similar untamed charisma, an Us vs The World rallying cry against soul-killing conformity.

At the same time, avoid the folly of rendering a mere two-dimensional bad boy cartoon devoid of pathos. Your readers must be enamored yet also gutted by your protagonist's perpetual alienation and cosmic loneliness, no matter how bright their spotlights blaze. All those raging chemicals and maniacal excesses fueling their artistry must emerge as flailing attempts at self-medicating some bottomless inner lack. Layer in psychosexual traumas, creative demons, and profound philosophies curdled by cynicism.

In essence, your rockstar can never be a hollow rockstar construct – they must manifest an undeniably human core aching to evolve, to love, to be satiated beyond the chemical oblivion pursuits of fame. What sort of childhood rubble forged their defensive armor and distrust toward vulnerability? What whispers from the abyss push them into escalating self-destructive excess just as success arrives? These are the dueling angelic and demonic energies that must permeate your larger-than-life conception to ring authentically torn.

Your anti-hero's inherent contradictions and dueling drives should manifest in every aspect of their characterization as well – from their belief systems to their most granular speech patterns and tastes. Gift them a compelling inner value system that wars with their hedonistic impulses, overlaying a rich spiritual curiosity atop their moody ennui. Invest them with compelling creative obsessions and eccentric academic fascinations outside of music that hint at their longing to evolve.

Make their voice and persona effervesce with a signature blend of romantic brooding, world-weary pragmatism, profound spirituality, and wickedly indulgent turns of phrase. A master of evocative poetry one moment and lovable jackass humor the next. An empath who can discern your greatest insecurities yet also knows exactly how to disarm you with raw seductive fire. An enraptured sage of creation's mysteries whose casual arrogance and vices still alienate them from their own deepest wisdom.

For antagonistic forces warring against your antihero's inner heroism, look no further than the parasitic industry leeches and toxic yes-men that inevitably attach to phenomenal success. Beyond the obvious demonic trifecta of narcotics, alcohol, and limitless indulgence, these corrosive human elements can turn your character's runaway rockstar id against themselves. Corporate gatekeepers who weaponize shame toward your artist's rawness. Weaselly managers stoking their most self-destructive proclivities. Society hangers-on mirroring the emptiest aspects of their ego to disastrous ends.

Conversely, there must exist a series of catalytic allies and sages who keep throwing your protagonist lifelines amid their voluptuous descent into excess. Bandmates and creative foils sworn to uphold their mutual pact toward achieving transcendent resonance together, no matter how many times they stumble. Awe-struck confidantes with hard-won wisdom offering knowing guidance. Most importantly, the saga's moral lodestar - the heroine destined to become an all-consuming obsession and cleansing flame for your antihero's toxic attachments.

For at their core, your rockstar's greatest superpower and fatal flaw must stem from the same source - their primal creative eros, their fire to transmute all of life's joys and tortures into the ravishing euphoria of true art and expression. It's the furnace that births their most rapturous amorous and spiritual awakenings...yet also the realm where their insatiable appetites toward carnal and chemical gratification can metastasize into narcissism meltdowns and existential despair.

Your rockstar protagonist must emerge as a tightrope walker choreographing a dizzying high-wire act between lacerating desecration and absolution. A haunted genius composed of equal parts spellbinding shamanic illumination and bad-boy charisma whose eternal war against their own excess achieves the grandeur of scripture. With one misstep risking a devastating swan dive, he must seduce and wound us through his grapple for grace while never losing that spark of divinity that first made us worship at his altar.

Chapter 5

Sculpting the Soulmate for Your Rockstar Deity

With your transcendent antihero forged in smoldering vitality, we turn to the crucial counterweight destined to become their all-consuming romantic obsession - the relatable "everywoman" heroine who will detonate their stubbornly walled-off heart. Just as your tortured musical idol must thrum with Byronic mythical grandeur tempered by harrowing vulnerabilities, their fated love interest must exist as the embodied dream fantasy and grounded reality check required to initiate their emotional rebirth.

For many authors, this woman often emerges as the inverse of the rockstar archetype's indulgent excesses and messianic self-absorption. She must radiate a groundedness, humility, and calming sensuality incongruent with her partner's raging tempest of reckless impulses and grandiose neuroses. Yet, to avoid flattening her into the cliché of a one-dimensional "calming influence," you must imbue her with a convincing inner depth and spiritual substance to both intrigue and subvert your antihero's roiling assumptions.

Rather than sculpting a meek, cowering figure overawed by their intended mythic radiance, invest your heroine with the unshakable self-possession and keen observational insight to both deflate and penetrate the rockstar's cynical facade. Anoint her with an impenetrable sense of independence and conviction to embark on her emotional evolution, yet allow her to wield patience and empathy like Aikido against your protagonist's storm of ego and angst.

While radically distinct from their intended on the outside, your heroine should, in many ways, reflect an exalted mirror of their mate's deepest soulful aspirations. As your prodigal's rutting, indulgent exterior obscures their aching essence; she must exemplify everything they long to rekindle - a purity of intent, a serenity, a wisdom anchored in timeless earthly and romantic ideals. Her luminous self-actualization acts as a seductive beacon and aggressive challenge to their growing existential void.

On a metaphysical level, your heroine should enter as your protagonist's ultimate "anima" - the primal feminine ideal personified, a willful embodiment of the Goddess energy capable of inspiring artistic raptures and shocking them out of toxic ego attachments. In her softness, vulnerability, and selfless grace, she wields the power to neutralize your antihero's most acidic nihilistic defenses while catalyzing their heroic inner valor to blaze forth in service of something greater finally.

Yet, to avoid the cliché of the corny "magical pixie dream

girl" archetype, you must ensure your heroine exists as a fully formed individual navigating complexities and contradictions of her own, not merely an idealized Madonna. Anoint her with a potent combination of wisdom and worldly experience that commands respect, a genuine erotic vitality that can match your prodigal's, and a lived-in human warmth that emanates hard-won growth more than blind purity.

Question her assumptions, equip her sharp wits and humor to disarm your cyclone's bluster, and flaws that make her relatable. Gift her compelling creative pursuits, her resilience earned from scars, and a rich inner ethics shaped by diverse communities outside your antihero's bubble. Make her at times admirably yet frustratingly stubborn and just as likely to test your hero's saintly patience as he is hers.

At her core, she should exude a profound emotional literacy and self-awareness - a fluent mastery of processing and communicating her inner storm in direct contrast to the compulsive evasions of your drifting muse. She soothes not via passive quietude but a deceptively passionate self-assuredness and the patience to repeatedly shatter their walled ignorance without destroying them. She is a supremely actualized figure who ultimately owns her desires, confidence, and transformational journey without needing salvation.

On a visceral level, your heroine's spirit animal persona should synergize and contrast their high-soaring beloveds. Suppose he manifests the reckless audacity and anarchic swagger of a libertine panther. In that case, he anoints her with a serpent spirit's grounded sensuality and sinuous mystery - an aura of ancient wisdom and sexuality that seductively entangles yet strikes with reasonable precision. A silky, understated magnetism and self-possession that unassumingly steals every scene and shatters his dismissive male arrogance.

Your heroine is a magnetic channel through which your raging antihero witnesses both the healing catharsis of unconditional love and the petrifying surrender required to earn its ultimate fulfillment. Make no mistake - even as her irresistible allure short-circuits their cynical defenses, she must embody the quiet yet unconquerable will to demand brutal honesty, self-actualization, and non-negotiable reciprocal devotion in exchange for her rapturous embrace.

She should terrorize their anti-social lone wolf instincts with her unwavering insistence on radical intimacy and extricating them from erotic and spiritual isolation. Seduce them with the possibility of life-altering communion while wielding the power to plunge them back into their blackest existential void with a single unreturned phone call. As their dance deepens, she becomes the all-encompassing muse and ultimate emotional Everest they must confront or perish inside their gilded fortress of solipsism.

More than merely saving a tortured auteur from themselves, your heroine's role is detonating their evolution from tragically alienated creative outcast toward an integrated human being capable of embodying their own hard-won wisdom and rejoining the greater soul collective. Through her feminine mystique - the nourishing tide of emotional intelligence, sensual power, and compassionate authority -

she coaxes the exiled god back home to their divine core truths.

Whether she emerges from your protagonist's inner orbit or blindsides them from an unanticipated realm, your heroine must immolate as their gravitational lodestar realizes. Over the breathless nights spent naked in revelatory soul exchange, she becomes both the muse unlocking his exalted creative plane and the transcendent beloved awakening them to the raptures lying far beyond carnal and narcissistic ego pursuits. To end their cyclical limbo, she demands nothing less than their unconditional surrender and every last shred of their authentic humanity laid bare.

Chapter 6

Bringing your Rock Circus Entourage to Life

With your fated romantic leads now burning in vivid distinction, your attention turns toward populating their high-voltage world with a rich supporting cast of eccentrics and catalysts. The wildly unpredictable gaggle of backup singers, hellion bandmates, opportunistic freeloaders, and ruthless industry parasites orbiting your respective heroes will transform their tale from a duet into a grand rock opera spectacle.

Let's start with those closest to your protagonist's smoldering heart and creative co-conspirators - their fellow musicians forging the aural alchemy together through sublime highs and shambolic lows alike. In Elizabeth Hunter's hallowed Wicked Beat series spanning Shredded, Double-bassed, and Tunedrummer, Ash's turbulent relationships with bandmates like Kris, Braden, and Shane contributed as much delicious friction and emotional catharsis as his central romance itself.

You have ample opportunities to play when conceptualizing these quasi-siblings bound by a pact written in distortion and poetic reverence. They could manifest as dysfunctional family members waging passive-aggressive cold wars while crafting stadium anthems. Hedonistic maniacs hellbent on making every quiet room a bonfire of substance-saturated bacchanalia. Or perhaps truly enlightened souls who've transmuted their wounds into renegade gospels only they can hear.

Regardless of their specific archetype, these brothers and sisters in noise should emerge as simultaneously your lead's most steadfast allies and merciless wolf pack of emotional button-pushers. They're the only cohorts able to wound your protagonist as savagely as they can elevate them, making them dangerous instigators on their intended romantic journey toward integration as much as anchoring creative co-pilots.

For maximum impact, imbue each bandmate with a compellingly lopsided approach toward romance, ambition, and bodily appetites - essentially their personification of whichever metaphysical ideal or human failing your protagonist and their heroine orbit around. The bawdy Falstaffian satyr, the draconian scenery-devouring narcissist, the incurable free spirit lost in perpetual childlike wanderlust, the wounded shaman - let their dysfunctions and quests mirror yet pervert the central drama's deeper questions about desire, freedom, self-actualization, and meaning.

So, for example, in Olivia Cunning's *Sinners on Tour* saga, the band of debauched anti-heroes stomping through novels like *Rock Hard* and *Hot Ticket* embodied lust, vice, and reckless pleasure taken to their most chaotic edges - providing a demented circus mirror of cautionary reflections for the central couple. In many ways, they gave human form to all the unrestrained carnal ids that Cunning's romantic leads needed to confront and integrate into wisdom.

On the other end of the spectrum, Rose Lerner used her surprise hit *Shake It Off* to populate the supporting ensemble around her rockstar hero with nurturing yet sharply insightful mentors and muses. Tender trainwreck Jorin's bandmates and support team emerged as the surrogate family cluster's respective voices of patience, tough love, and healing compassion - simultaneously forging the alchemical container for his eventual transformation while never shying from harsh truths about addiction and arrested development strangling his gifts.

Now, let's pivot outside your band's touring juggernaut and dive into the gnarled underworld of industry leeches preying upon your larger-than-life co's narcissistic vulnerabilities and unchecked impulses. For every timeless vampire producer like Jade's insidious svengali Roscoe Vance in Penelope Ward's *Room Hate* determined to drain their exploited cash cows of integrity, you'll need a spectrum of sycophants and spin-doctors masquerading as advisers.

There's the eternally sketched-out personal assistant perpetually hosing down PR flare-ups and mitigating collateral damage, a starkly pragmatic tour manager ruthlessly devoted to the bottom line, and, of course, the parasitic lawyer whispering in their ear to disregard all virtues beyond pleasure, profit, and brand extension. Each should exert their insidious gravity, warping your protagonist's morals, challenging your heroine to stay anchored amidst the maelstrom around their lover.

On the redemptive inverse, assembling a crew of grounded, creative allies fighting in your core couple's corner is just as vital. Perhaps a Zen recording technician embodying the laidback mindfulness so foreign to your male ego stud. An earthy spiritual guru trying to coax them toward transcendent breakthroughs beyond the material and corporeal. A fatherly manager long since disenchanted by the hedonism yet still carrying their duty like Atlas.

In Erika Kelly's devastating Rock Star Romance trilogy, these nurturing presences counterbalanced the darkness - from heroines' bromide bandmates to reliable father figures escorting them into healthier habits. By rendering these protectors in a tender yet uncompromising distinction from the snakes and yes-men, Kelly reinforced why her rockstar antiheroes must evolve or wither entirely on the vine.

Meanwhile, J. Kenner's massive hit *Fallen* catalyzed suspense and interpersonal landmines by depicting the extended family - parents, half-siblings, and distant relatives harboring their own torturous entanglements with the rockstar's legacy. This tragic ouroboros of unresolved wounds, envy, and intimacies-gone-sour allowed for some of the genre's most electrifying slap-in-the-face wake-up calls regarding celebrity's corrosive toll on domestic bonds.

When stacked adequately around your romantic heroes, this circus of seducers and guardrails should embody macro and micro counterpoints to their evolution...or devolution. If left unchecked, do all these ravening ids, literal and figurative sycophants, and unavoidable emotional wreckage risk dragging them back into the oblivion of depravity? Or might each outrageous destabilizing force end up a perverse guardian angel pushing your leads toward integration, individuation, and mystical reunion despite themselves?

Chapter 7

Constructing Rockstar Worlds That Bleed Authenticity

While conjuring your tempestuous central figures from the creative ether, you must simultaneously craft an entire richly textured world around them - immersive alternate realms where your rockstar deities can transcend the mundane yet still feel grounded in gritty plausibility. The finely etched details of these environments will elevate your high-wire romantic fantasy into a bona fide escapist excursion readers can sink into viscerally.

Let's start with the most immediate sphere you'll need to render in true-to-life dynamism - the touring machinery of perpetual flux and indulgence churning around your band of mythic personae. From the dive bar dressing rooms reeking of spilled beer and coagulated makeup to the sleeper bus bunks where between-city romps and emotional breakdowns unspool, you must immerse us in the exhilarating yet grueling fishbowl existence of life on the road.

In her epic 'Sinners on Tour' series, Olivia Cunning

established herself as the master world-builder of rockstar touring life's most unvarnished extremities. Through uncompromisingly explicit tomes like 'Backstage Pass,' 'Rock Hard,' and 'Double Time,' she pulled no punches in transporting readers deep into the whirlwind of tour bus shag sessions, hotel room bacchanals, and the surreal alienation of waking up in a new city's anonymous room service Jacuzzi each dawn.

Not to be outdone, Penelope Ward's smash hit 'RoomHate' hurled us so deeply into the backstage circus that we almost caught a contact high. Right from the novel's iconic opening scene of a hotel room demolition amid dueling fits of megalomania and ecstasy, Ward's scorching eye for authentic detail encoded every grimace and bead of sweat amid the riotous tableau.

Of course, world-building the touring experience extends far beyond the mere technicalities of the road grind and its hedonistic rituals. You must also strive to encode the bone-deep paradoxes shaping your rockstar pantheon's unique psychologies when bouncing between celestial spotlights and earth-bound purgatorial spaces within hours of each other.

For a master class in capturing this dissonance, look no further than Erin Kern's lyrical magnum opus 'Permanent Obscurity'. Through her haunting protagonist Dirk Ashby, Kern made us feel the striking absurdity of vaulting between cosmic celebrations of the human spirit at arena shows, back into the mundanity of unmemorable airports and droning motorway hypnosis mere hours later. Her poetic rendering of the emotional whiplash endured en route to musical worship enacted its existential examination.

Similarly, Kylie Scott exhibited an almost anthropological level of nuance in depicting the rattling quotidian pains coexisting alongside rock raptures in her beloved 'Stage Dive' and 'Dive Bar' sagas. Her protagonists like David and Jimmy may have set our paperbacks aflame with their erotic feats. Yet, Scott crucially balanced the Dionysian dream against scenes that intensely memorialized human struggles like maintaining connections with exes, taxing travel regimens, and emotional flameouts behind velvet curtains.

Yet beyond capturing the touring gauntlet in all its seductive bombast and banality, you must strive to construct entire interconnected ecosystems within your plot's rock n' roll microcosms. From the corporate boardrooms where label execs cynically strategize exploiting their latest liabilities to the raucous festival grounds where the most zealous fans worship with unholy fervor, cultivate a vibrant living tapestry populated with archetypal figures as nuanced as your leads.

In books like 'Champagne' and 'Tease,' Jessica Hawkins proved herself an unrivaled world-builder, charting the entire interconnected realm of studios, radio stations, and industry machinery fueling and exploiting her tales. By immersing readers in the toxic Petri dishes where performers metamorphose from creative sparks into revenue-generating content delivery vectors, Hawkins infused even tertiary characters like radio personalities and label executives with rich inner lives, elevating them beyond caricature.

This ability to encode holistic labyrinths of interpersonal politics becomes especially vital if, like J. Kenner's masterworks 'Fallen Too Far' and 'Fall For Me', your story scrutinizes how rockstardom radiates outward in concentric circles of relational damage. Kenner's tales of addiction and psychological trauma rippling across generations of a music dynasty demanded vividly rendering everything from gossipy crew anecdotes to seamy celebrity hospital accounts.

On the other side of the rockstar world spectrum, Rose Lerner saturated her grounded yet soulful novel 'Shake It Off' with such deeply researched ethnographic attunement to the indie/punk underground that you could practically smell the zine trading and hear the impassioned slice-of-life diatribes unfolding on Petersburg's back-alley stages. By making her lower-register rockstar poet feel like more than a punchline, Lerner infused every scuffed basement and acoustic guitar pull with philosophical weight.

Stepping outside the immediate orbit of creative satellites and industry machines, you must also conjure realistic civic backdrops where the most pivotal junctures of your anti-heroes' journeys unravel in surprising locales. From the glitzy Manhattan penthouses hosting champagne-soaked afterparties to the desert highways where psychic breakdowns paralyze tour momentum, immerse us in the vividly-etched settings functioning as proving grounds for grand romantic epiphanies or cataclysmic unravelings.

Nowhere did this interplay of geographical spheres shape-shifting between refuge, battlefield, and initiation chambers emerge more vividly than Kylie Scott's riotous

'Lead.' Whether dragging us from civil war zones of overindulgence like Berlin's hedonistic techno lairs into the oasis-like clarity of Nova Scotia's wintry solitude, Scott masterfully juxtaposed complementary arena rockscalating tensions while paradoxically setting the stage for emotional catharsis.

When striving for this degree of fully enclosed world-building, A.J. Renee's moody St. Delyn series provides an enlightening blueprint. By interweaving intricately researched New Orleans civic tapestries into her dissections of rock n' roll's underworld corruption, Renee accomplished the nifty trick of making her shadowy Big Easy locales feel like a Greek chorus commenting directly on the central dramas unspooling. Her soaked urban vignettes enriched melodramatic themes about creative integrity and moral dilemmas through resonant symbolic framing.

Ultimately, whether rendering decadent hotel orgies or thoughtfully overturning rocks to expose the grit under-neath, the key to conjuring an authentic rockstar existence lies in diligently studying the ultra-scene's most minute textures and contradictions from every conceivable angle. Because transporting readers into these heightened realms of indulgence and creative communion requires a complete accounting - the sensuality of sumptuous textures, the reek of sweat and vices, the chiaroscuro of lofty mind-expansion followed by mundane ego-puncturing...and vice versa again in an infinite Möbius coil.

Only once you breathe living, pulsing dynamism into every corner of the demimonde can your feverishly wrought central characters feel like mere avatars through which larger archetypal forces are battling for the rockstar soul. For better or worse, they exist as brave explorers breaching ever-shifting frontiers - and we must experience their entire dizzying spheres of navigation without a single thread of illusion fraying.

Chapter 8

Romantic Tension (Slow Burn vs Instant Attraction)

Creating steamy romantic tension is key to writing a bestselling rockstar romance. You want your readers to feel the electricity between your characters, whether a slow-burn romance that gradually builds or an instant attraction that ignites from the moment they meet. Let's explore how you can craft these dynamic relationships in your story.

First, let's briefly discuss slow-burn romances (we'll dive deeper into this subject in the next chapter). In this type of story, the attraction between your rockstar and their love interest grows over time. It's a delicious dance of longing glances, accidental touches, and flirtatious banter. Think of it like the song 'Slow Hands' by Niall Horan—the anticipation builds with each verse until it reaches a satisfying crescendo.

You need to establish the initial spark between your characters to create a compelling slow-burn romance. Maybe it's a chance encounter at a concert or a shared passion for music. From there, you can gradually increase the tension through shared moments and obstacles that keep them apart. In 'Lick' by Kylie Scott, the heroine wakes up married to a famous rockstar after a wild night in Vegas. As they navigate their unexpected relationship, their attraction grows until it's impossible to ignore.

On the other hand, instant attraction can be just as thrilling in a rockstar romance. This is when your characters feel an immediate and undeniable pull toward each other, like two magnets snapping together. It's the kind of chemistry that makes your heart race and your palms sweat. In Kristen Callihan's 'Idol,' the heroine falls into the arms of her celebrity crush, sparking an intense and passionate relationship.

When writing instant attraction, it's important to make it believable. You can't just tell your readers that your characters are attracted to each other - you have to show it through their actions and reactions. Describe how their eyes lock across a crowded room or how their skin tingles when they accidentally brush against each other. In 'Rock Hard' by Nalini Singh, the heroine is the only one who isn't intimidated by the rockstar hero's gruff exterior. Their banter is electric from the start, and it's clear that there's a powerful attraction simmering beneath the surface.

Whether you choose a slow-burn or instant attraction, the key is to keep the tension high throughout your story. You can introduce obstacles that keep your characters apart, such as misunderstandings, external conflicts, or personal baggage. In 'Rockstar' by Lauren Rowe, the hero pushes the heroine away because he thinks he's not good enough for her.

The push-and-pull of their relationship keeps readers on the edge of their seats.

Another way to build tension is through physical proximity. Put your characters in situations where they can't avoid each other, like a cramped tour bus or a secluded recording studio. Describe how their bodies react to being close together - the racing heartbeats and shivers down their spines. In 'Lead' by Kylie Scott, the heroine is forced to share a hotel room with the rockstar hero, leading to a night of intense sexual tension.

You can also use music to heighten the romantic tension in your story. Have your characters bond over a love of a particular song or album. In 'The Might Have Been' by Shay Savage, the hero and heroine connect over their mutual appreciation for classic rock. Or, use lyrics to express your characters' emotions but can't quite put into words.

Remember, the goal is to make your readers feel the same butterflies and anticipation that your characters are experiencing. Use sensory details to bring the tension to life on the page. Describe how the hero's fingers feel as they brush against the heroine's skin or how her breath catches in her throat when he leans in close.

Another tip is to use secondary characters to ramp up the tension. Have your heroine's best friend tease her about her crush on the rockstar, or have the hero's bandmate give him a hard time about his feelings for the heroine. In 'Rock Courtship' by Nalini Singh, the hero's bandmates constantly rib him about his attraction to the heroine, adding more tension to their interactions.

Finally, don't be afraid to let the tension build to a breaking point. There's nothing more satisfying than a well-earned kiss or a passionate declaration of love after chapters of simmering attraction. In 'Dirty' by Kylie Scott, the hero and heroine finally surrender their feelings after a night of intense flirting and almost-kisses. The payoff is electric and well worth the wait.

In conclusion, crafting sizzling romantic tension is essential for writing a bestselling rockstar romance. Whether you opt for a slow burn or instant attraction, use sensory details, obstacles, proximity, music, and secondary characters to keep the tension high throughout your story. With these tips in mind, your readers will swoon and eagerly turn the pages to see what happens next.

Chapter 9

Slow Burn

Slow burn is a crucial element in rockstar romances that adds depth, anticipation, and emotional intensity to the story. It's the gradual buildup of tension and attraction between the main characters, often spanning multiple obstacles and conflicts before they finally give in to their desires.

One of the primary roles of slow burn in rockstar romances is to create a palpable sense of longing and chemistry between the characters. For instance, in Carian Cole's 'Ashes to Ink,' the connection between the lead guitarist and the heroine simmers beneath the surface for a significant portion of the book, with each stolen glance and accidental touch amplifying the sexual tension.

Slow burn also allows for character development and growth. As the characters navigate their feelings and the challenges posed by their respective lifestyles, they undergo transformations that make their eventual union more meaningful and satisfying. In Kylie Scott's Lick, the hero's journey from a commitment-phobic rockstar to a man willing to open his heart is a pivotal aspect of the slow-burn narrative.

Moreover, slow burn adds an element of realism to rockstar romances. Musicians' lifestyles often involve constant touring, media scrutiny, and temptations, making it challenging to sustain a stable relationship. The gradual progression of the romantic arc in books like Kristen Callihan's 'Managed' reflects the real-world obstacles faced by couples in the music industry.

Slow burn can also heighten the emotional impact of the story. By delaying the gratification of the characters' desires, the reader becomes invested in their journey, rooting for them to overcome the obstacles and find their way to each other. K.A. Tucker's 'Until It Fades' exemplifies this, with the slow burn building to a powerful climax that resonates deeply with readers.

Another role of slow burn in rockstar romances is to create a sense of anticipation and suspense. As the tension between the characters escalates, the reader becomes increasingly invested in their eventual union, eagerly turning pages to witness the moment when they finally succumb to their attraction. Terri Anne Browning's 'The Rocker' series masterfully employs this technique, keeping readers on the edge of their seats.

Slow burn can also add depth to the characters' emotional journeys. As they navigate their feelings and confront their fears and vulnerabilities, the characters often undergo personal growth and self-discovery. Nalini Singh's 'Rock Courtship' beautifully portrays this aspect, with the hero's journey towards self-acceptance and the heroine's struggle to overcome her past traumas woven into the slow-burn dynamic.

Furthermore, slow burn can enhance the sense of authenticity in rockstar romances. The demanding schedules and the pressure of fame can make it challenging for musicians to form meaningful connections. The gradual development of romantic relationships in books like Toni Aleo's 'The Vaughan Family series' reflects the real-world challenges those in the music industry face.

Slow burn can also create a sense of nostalgia and longing for those who have experienced the intensity of a slow-burning romance. As readers follow the characters' journey, they may be reminded of their romantic experiences, adding an extra layer of emotional resonance to the story. Lexi Blake's 'Courted by Scandal' captures this nostalgia beautifully, evoking memories of the thrill of a slow-burning courtship.

Moreover, slow burn can serve as a commentary on societal expectations and gender roles. As the characters navigate their feelings and confront the pressures of their respective lifestyles, they may challenge traditional norms and expectations. Penelope Douglas's 'Bully' series explores this aspect, with the slow burn dynamic reflecting the characters' struggles against societal constraints.

Additionally, slow burn can add depth to the supporting characters and their roles in the overall story. As the main characters navigate their feelings, the secondary characters often play crucial roles in providing guidance, support, or obstacles to the budding romance. Kylie Scott's 'Stage Dive' series is a prime example, with the band members and their relationships contributing to the slow burn dynamic.

Lastly, slow burn can create a sense of anticipation and excitement for future installments in a series. Authors can effectively build a dedicated fanbase that eagerly awaits the next book by leaving readers craving for more after witnessing the characters' emotional journey. Kristen Callihan's 'VIP' series is a testament to the power of slow burn in creating a loyal following.

Chapter 10

Instant Attraction

Instant attraction is pivotal in rockstar romances. It ignites the initial spark between the characters and sets the stage for an intense and passionate love story. This immediate connection catalyzes the romance, propelling the characters into a whirlwind of desire and emotion.

In Kylie Scott's Lick, the instant attraction between the lead singer of a rock band and a young woman he encounters at a party is palpable from their first meeting. Their electric chemistry is undeniable, setting the tone for the sizzling romance throughout the book.

Instant attraction can also be a powerful source of conflict in rockstar romances. When characters find themselves inexplicably drawn to someone they perceive as off-limits or unsuitable, it creates delicious tension that keeps readers hooked. Kristen Callihan's 'Managed' explores this dynamic, with the heroine struggling to resist her instant attraction to the brooding rockstar she's been hired to manage.

Moreover, instant attraction can add a sense of urgency and intensity to the romantic storyline. When an overwhelming desire from the outset consumes characters, it can lead to impulsive actions and high-stakes scenarios that keep the plot moving at a breakneck pace. Nalini Singh's 'Rock Courtship' exemplifies this, with the instant attraction between the rockstar and the heroine igniting a passionate and tumultuous affair.

Instant attraction can also set the stage for personal growth and self-discovery. As characters grapple with intense feelings, they may be forced to confront their fears, insecurities, and past traumas, leading to powerful character development. Terri Anne Browning's 'The Rocker' series explores this aspect, with the heroes' instant attraction to their love interests prompting them to reevaluate their priorities and embrace vulnerability.

Furthermore, instant attraction can create a sense of escapism and fantasy for readers. The idea of an immediate and all-consuming connection with a charismatic rockstar appeals to our romantic ideals, allowing us to vicariously experience the thrill and excitement of such a passionate encounter. Toni Aleo's 'The Vaughan Family' series taps into this fantasy, offering readers a tantalizing glimpse into the lives of rockstars and their whirlwind romances.

Instant attraction can also add a layer of complexity to the characters' emotional journeys. When characters face intense feelings from the outset, they must navigate the challenges of balancing their desires with their responsibilities, values, and commitments. K.A. Tucker's 'Until It Fades' explores this aspect, with the heroine struggling to reconcile her instant attraction to a rockstar with her sense of duty and loyalty.

Moreover, instant attraction can serve as a reflection of the high-stakes, adrenaline-fueled lifestyle of rockstars. The intensity and passion that characterize their music and performances often spill over into their personal lives, leading to intense and all-consuming romantic connections. Lexi Blake's 'Courted by Scandal' captures this essence, with the instant attraction between the characters mirroring the raw energy and intensity of the rock world.

Additionally, instant attraction can create a sense of excitement and anticipation for readers. When characters experience an immediate and undeniable connection, it sets the stage for a rollercoaster of emotions and events, keeping readers eagerly turning pages to see how the romance will unfold. Penelope Douglas's 'Bully' series capitalizes on this anticipation, with the instant attraction between the main characters igniting a firestorm of passion and drama.

Instant attraction can also serve as a commentary on the power of physical chemistry and primal desire. In a world where appearances and superficial attraction often take precedence, rockstar romances can explore the depth and complexity of these intense physical connections, challenging societal norms and expectations. Kristen Callihan's 'VIP' series delves into this aspect, with the instant attraction between the characters serving as a backdrop for deeper explorations of desire, vulnerability, and intimacy.

Furthermore, instant attraction can add an element of unpredictability and spontaneity to the narrative. When characters are swept up in the intensity of their emotions, it can lead to unexpected twists and turns, keeping readers guessing and invested in the story's outcome. Carian Cole's 'Ashes to Ink' exemplifies this, with the instant attraction between the lead characters driving a series of impulsive decisions and dramatic events.

Lastly, instant attraction can create a sense of immediacy and urgency in the romance, mirroring the fast-paced and high-stakes world of the music industry. When an overwhelming desire from the outset consumes characters, it adds a sense of urgency and intensity to their romantic journey, reflecting the whirlwind nature of life on the road and in the spotlight. Kylie Scott's 'Stage Dive' series captures this essence, with the instant attraction between the characters propelling them into a passionate and intense love affair that defies convention.

Chapter 11

Steam

You find yourself swept up in the whirlwind world of rockstar romances, where passion burns as bright as the stage lights. The air crackles with electricity as you lose yourself in the pages, immersed in the steamy encounters that unfold between your favorite characters. Every caress, every heated gaze sends a delicious shiver racing down your spine, leaving you craving more.

In 'Rocked' by Cari Quinn and Taryn Elliott, the heat level rises as the lead singer pins his love interest against the wall, his lips trailing a scorching path down her neck. Their breaths mingle, heavy with desire, as they surrender to the undeniable chemistry that has been simmering between them. His skilled hands roam her curves, eliciting soft gasps and whimpers as he claims her in a heated embrace, the world around them fading into insignificance.

The dressing room becomes a sanctuary of forbidden

pleasure in 'Rock Hard' by Nalini Singh. You can almost feel the rough texture of the velvet curtains against your skin as the rockstar's calloused fingers blaze a path of fire, eliciting gasps and whimpers from his lover's parted lips. The air grows thick with the heady scent of desire as he trails scorching kisses along the column of her throat, his every touch igniting a conflagration of need.

In 'Backstage Pass' by Olivia Cunning, the heated encounters have a deliciously voyeuristic edge. The heavy bass line thrums through your veins as you bear witness to the lead guitarist's skilled fingers working their magic, coaxing pleasure from his lover's trembling body. Her back arches in ecstasy as he worships her with his lips and hands, leaving no inch of her skin unexplored.

The tour bus becomes a mobile oasis of passion in 'On the Road' by Lexi Blake. You can almost taste the heady scent of desire mingling with the faint aroma of leather as the rockstar claims his lover's lips in a searing kiss, their bodies entwined in a tangle of limbs and heated caresses. The world outside fades away as they lose themselves in the intoxicating rhythm of their bodies moving as one.

In 'Tempting Beat' by Gwendolyn Harleth, the dressing room mirror reflects the sensual dance of two lovers, their bodies moving in perfect rhythm. You can almost hear the ragged breaths and whispered endearments as they lose themselves in the intoxicating ebb and flow of pleasure. His talented fingers find secret erogenous zones, coaxing forth gasps and sighs of pure bliss that echo off the walls.

The heat level in 'Rock Rebel' by Tara Leigh soars as the

brooding frontman claims his lover with a possessive hunger. You can practically feel the scorching trail his lips blaze across her heated skin, igniting a conflagration of desire that consumes them both. His touch is branding, searing her flesh with the intensity of his need as they surrender to the flames of passion.

In 'Rock Addiction' by Nalini Singh, the electrifying energy of the stage spills over into the bedroom, where the lead guitarist's nimble fingers pluck a different kind of melody from his lover's body. The air grows thick with the heady scent of sweat and desire, leaving you breathless. Her back arches in ecstasy as he coaxes her higher and higher, their cries of pleasure a symphony in the night.

The backstage area becomes a sultry playground in 'Rock Courtship' by Olivia Cunning. You can almost taste the irresistible blend of lipstick and whiskey as the rockstar's tongue dances across his lover's lips, igniting an inferno of passion that threatens to consume them both. The heat between them is searing, their bodies moving in a primal rhythm as old as time itself.

In 'Rock Me' by Michelle Mankin, the hotel room becomes a sanctuary of forbidden delights. The crisp sheets whisper against heated skin as the bassist's skilled hands map every curve and contour of his lover's body, coaxing forth gasps and sighs of pure ecstasy. The world outside fades away as they lose themselves in the intoxicating dance of desire, chasing that elusive pinnacle of bliss.

The dimly lit bar sets the stage for a heated encounter in 'Rock Revival' by Lexi Blake. You can practically feel the heat radiating off their bodies as the frontman's fingers tangle in his lover's hair, drawing her into a searing kiss that promises untold pleasures. The air grows thick with the heady scent of desire as they surrender to the flames of passion, consequences be damned.

In 'Rock Solid' by Nalini Singh, the dressing room mirror reflects the sinful dance of two lovers, their bodies moving in perfect sync. The air grows thick with the heady scent of desire as the rockstar's skilled hands explore every inch of his lover's trembling form. Her breathy moans echo off the walls as he pushes her higher and higher until the world around them shatters into a kaleidoscope of pure ecstasy.

The rooftop becomes a forbidden oasis in 'Rock Me Harder' by Olivia Cunning. The city lights twinkle below as the lead guitarist claims his lover's lips in a searing kiss, their bodies moving in a heated rhythm that defies the cool night air. His touch is branding, scorching a path of fire across her sensitive skin as she arches against him, craving more of his exquisite torture.

In 'Rock Star' by Tara Leigh, the heat level soars as the frontman pins his lover against the wall, his tongue tracing a scorching path down her neck. The air grows thick with the heady scent of desire, leaving you breathless and craving more. Her nails rake down his back as he claims her with a possessive hunger, their bodies moving in a primal dance as old as time itself.

The dimly lit alleyway becomes a sultry playground in 'Rock Hard' by Nalini Singh. The rough brick scratches against heated skin as the bassist's skilled hands map every curve and contour of his lover's body, eliciting gasps and whimpers of pure ecstasy. The world around them fades away as they surrender to the flames of passion, lost in a haze of desire and the intoxicating scent of sweat and sin.

Chapter 12

Conflicts & Struggles

As you develop your rockstar character, consider the various external and internal conflicts they face on their journey. External conflicts with bandmates, rivals, the media, and the music industry itself can create compelling drama and tension. For example, in Kylie Scott's Lick, the hero David faces conflict with his band and management when a drunken marriage derails his career plans. Showing how your rockstar navigates these professional challenges will be key to their character arc.

Don't neglect your rockstar's internal conflicts and personal demons, either. Many rockstars struggle with substance abuse, as with the hero Killian in Jaine Diamond's 'Dirty Like Me' who battles alcoholism. Depicting their vices and addictions realistically, as well as the hard work of overcoming them, will make the rockstar feel more human and relatable. Other personal struggles like anxiety, depression, childhood trauma, or anger issues can also shape a rockstar character in exciting ways.

Fame and life in the spotlight take a toll on rockstars and their relationships. Paparazzi, tabloid rumors, obsessive fans, and the pressure to maintain a particular image can all strain a romance. In Bella Andre's 'Wild In Love,' the rockstar hero's fame makes the heroine wary of dating him. Consider how your rockstar and their love interest handle the unique challenges of celebrity coupledom.

Another common obstacle is the rockstar's demanding tour schedule and long separations from home. Like Nalini Singh's 'Rock Addiction,' many rock romances portray the couple struggling to carve out quality time together amidst hectic travel and performances. Think about how stolen moments, brief tour visits from the love interest, and remote communication via text/phone can enhance the yearning and build anticipation until the couple's reunion.

Trust issues and fear of commitment also commonly plague rockstar characters. Justified or not, the "bad boy" reputation and groupie culture surrounding many rockstars can be a significant sore point in relationships. In Olivia Cunning's 'Backstage Pass,' the hero's history of casual hookups initially drives the heroine away. Jealousy over exes, misunderstandings, and secrets uncovered from the rockstar's past can all cause tensions for the couple to resolve.

A harrowing past betrayal, like a cheating ex, may have left deep emotional scars that make the rockstar reluctant to risk their heart again. The heroine of Mercy Brown's 'Loud Is How

I Love You' has vowed never to date a musician again after getting burned. A rockstar who someone has used for money, fame, or career advancement may now be cynical about love. Showing these vulnerable moments and the process of the rockstar learning to open up and trust again will be decisive.

Many romances also portray a rockstar hero clashing with the heroine's disapproving family or friends who consider him a bad influence. In Lita Ford's memoir, 'Living Like a Runaway,' Ford describes her parents' vehement opposition to her joining a rock band as a teenager in the 1970s. While attitudes have progressed somewhat, a certain stigma about the rock lifestyle persists in some circles. Seeing the couple prove the naysayers wrong can be very satisfying.

Power imbalances and different social circles can also cause friction. A younger or less successful heroine may feel insecure and worry the rockstar will ultimately prefer someone more on his level. The supermodel ex who unexpectedly shows up on tour, the flirtatious backup dancer, and the pushy groupie posting compromising photos - create obstacles that play on those anxieties and force the rockstar to prove his commitment.

Consider giving the rockstar and love interest careers, hobbies, or core values that sometimes clash. Perhaps the paparazzi fallout from their relationship jeopardizes an otherwise private person's job. Maybe the rockstar's outrageous onstage antics make the straitlaced heroine uncomfortable. The free-spirited rocker and the heroine determined to settle down may face conflicts over children and the future. Friction between their respective worlds creates juicy drama.

Beware of vilifying the press and public as one-dimensional enemies, though. Most people working in media do their jobs, while fans are the lifeblood of any rockstar's career. Showing some sympathetic press allies and enthusiastic supporters is more realistic than an army of haters. The rockstar's publicist desperately does damage control after an embarrassing scandal, and the earnest rookie reporter is nervous about interviewing their idol. These secondary characters can provide some comic relief amidst heavier external conflicts.

Consider also how sudden, unearned fame can be an obstacle if a talented amateur rockets to stardom after a single viral video. The whiplash of adjusting to a new lifestyle, the pressure to follow up a hit, frustration with being pigeonholed, and a nagging sense of impostor syndrome - explore how overnight celebrity impacts the rockstar's psyche and relationships. In L.J. Shen's 'Midnight Blue,' the hero's unexpected popularity on a singing competition show leads to inner turmoil.

A serious creative slump or losing joy in music altogether can be a major existential crisis for rockstars who have always made art their reason for being. Writer's block, feeling trapped in a confining genre or image, yearning to explore a different sound that clashes with what fans or record labels demand - these professional dilemmas can bleed into the rockstar's personal life, too. In Mercy Brown's 'Loud Is How I Love You,' the hero's struggle to write new music nearly derails his career and relationship.

Finally, consider how success and wealth impact the rockstar's core identity, values, and personal ties to home. Loyalty versus "selling out," balancing artistic integrity with commercial considerations, staying true to their roots while embracing a new reality - many rock romances explore these themes. The hero of Olivia Cunning's 'Backstage Pass' feels conflicted about hiding his working-class background to fit a rock god image. Protagonists who overcome various obstacles and find ways to remain authentic are highly compelling.

Chapter 13

Balancing Love and Rockin'

In rockstar romance stories, a common conflict arises when the rockstar's fame and lifestyle clash with their desire for a normal relationship. 'In 'Lick' by Kylie Scott,' the protagonist's fame creates a barrier in the budding relationship as the love interest struggles to navigate the world of constant scrutiny and public attention. This conflict adds tension and drama to the romance as the rockstar must find a way to balance their public persona with their private desires. The internal struggle of the rockstar torn between fame and personal happiness creates a compelling obstacle for the couple to overcome.

Another conflict rockstars face in romance stories revolves around maintaining trust and fidelity in the face of constant temptation and opportunities for infidelity. 'In 'Lead Me Back' by CD Reiss,' the protagonist's past relationships and image as a rockstar complicate their efforts to build a solid foundation with their love interest, leading to doubts and insecurities. This struggle to remain faithful and committed despite the allure of fame and other potential romantic interests adds depth to the story and tests the strength of the couple's bond. Overcoming this obstacle requires honest communication, self-reflection, and a deep commitment to each other.

A recurring theme in rockstar romance narratives is the conflict arising from the rockstar's past traumas and emotional baggage, which can hinder their ability to engage in a new relationship fully. 'In 'Idol' by Kristen Callihan,' the protagonist's troubled past and inner demons create barriers to intimacy and connection with their love interest, leading to misunderstandings and hurt feelings. This emotional conflict adds complexity to the story as the rockstar grapples with their past while trying to embrace a future with their partner. Overcoming these personal obstacles requires patience, understanding, and a willingness to confront and heal from past wounds.

The pressure to maintain a public image and meet fans' expectations can also create conflicts for rockstars in romance stories, as balancing personal desires with professional obligations becomes increasingly challenging. 'In 'Rock Wedding' by Nalini Singh,' the protagonist faces the dilemma of choosing between their career and their relationship, leading to tensions and sacrifices. This conflict highlights the sacrifices and compromises that rockstars often make to pursue their passion while navigating the complexities of love and relationships. The struggle to find a harmonious balance between fame, love, and personal fulfillment adds depth and realism to the story, resonating with readers who appreciate nuanced character dynamics.

In rockstar romance narratives, conflicts often arise from misunderstandings and miscommunications between the rockstar and their love interest, fueling the drama and tension in the story. 'In 'Backstage Pass' by Olivia Cunning,' the protagonist's inability to effectively communicate their feelings and intentions leads to confusion and discord in the relationship, jeopardizing their chance at happiness. This conflict underscores the importance of open and honest communication in fostering trust and understanding between the characters as they navigate the complexities of love amidst the chaos of fame and fortune. Overcoming these communication barriers requires vulnerability, empathy, and a willingness to listen and learn from each other's perspectives.

The clash between the rockstar's wild, rebellious image and their desire for stability and love often serves as a central conflict in rockstar romance tales, highlighting the internal struggle between past personas and present desires. 'In 'Dirty Like Me' by Jaine Diamond,' the protagonist's rockstar persona and reputation as a bad boy create obstacles in their pursuit of a meaningful and lasting relationship, forcing them to confront their own identity and values. This conflict explores themes of self-discovery and transformation as the rockstar grapples with their past choices and seeks redemption in love. Overcoming this internal conflict requires introspection, growth, and a willingness to embrace vulnerability and authenticity.

The pressure to constantly tour, perform, and meet the demands of a hectic schedule can create conflicts for rockstars in romance stories, as the rigors of their profession strain their relationships and challenge their ability to prioritize love. 'In 'Lost in Rewind' by Tali Alexander,' the protagonist's demanding career and touring commitments take a toll on their relationship, leading to misunderstandings and distance between them and their love interest. This conflict highlights rockstars' sacrifices and challenges as they strive to balance their passion for music with the demands of a romantic partnership. Overcoming this obstacle requires understanding, compromise, and a mutual commitment to weathering the storms together.

The clash between the rockstar's need for independence and their longing for connection and intimacy often serves as a key conflict in rockstar romance narratives, exploring the tension between individuality and partnership. 'In 'Rock Hard' by Nalini Singh,' the protagonist's fear of vulnerability and reliance on self-sufficiency hinder their ability to commit to their love interest fully, creating barriers to emotional intimacy and trust. This conflict delves into themes of fear of abandonment and opening up to love as the rockstar grapples with their insecurities and defense mechanisms. Overcoming this internal conflict requires courage, self-awareness, and a willingness to take emotional risks for the sake of love.

Family expectations and obligations can also present conflicts for rockstars in romance stories, as the pressure to meet familial responsibilities and live up to legacy collide with personal desires and ambitions. 'In 'Lost in You' by

Laurelin Paige,' the protagonist's strained relationship with their family and the expectations placed upon them by their upbringing create obstacles in their pursuit of happiness with their love interest, testing their resolve and independence. This conflict adds complexity to the narrative as the rockstar navigates familial ties and personal aspirations, grappling with the need to forge their path while honoring their roots. Overcoming this conflict requires courage, authenticity, and a willingness to redefine relationships on one's terms.

The clash between the rockstar's desire for anonymity and their public persona often serves as a central conflict in rockstar romance tales, exploring the tension between the private self and the public image. 'In 'Rock Addiction' by Nalini Singh,' the protagonist's reluctance to embrace their rockstar status and the constant scrutiny that comes with it creates obstacles in their budding relationship, leading to misunderstandings and anxiety. This conflict delves into themes of identity and self-acceptance as the rockstar grapples with their perception of fame and the expectations placed upon them by the public. Overcoming this internal conflict requires introspection, self-confidence, and a commitment to being true to oneself amidst the pressures of fame.

The battle between the past and the future often serves as a central conflict in rockstar romance narratives, as the protagonist grapples with old wounds and unresolved issues that threaten to derail their chance at love and happiness. 'In 'Rock Star' by Stacey Kennedy,' the protagonist's haunted past and the demons that continue to haunt them create barriers in their relationship with their love interest, fueling doubts and insecurities. This conflict delves into themes of forgiveness and healing as the rockstar confronts their past traumas and seeks redemption through love. Overcoming this emotional conflict requires resilience, vulnerability, and a willingness to confront and overcome one's darkest fears.

The clash between the rockstar's desire for freedom and their need for commitment and security often serves as a key conflict in rockstar romance narratives, exploring the tension between independence and partnership. 'In 'Rock King' by Tara Leigh,' the protagonist's fear of losing themselves in a relationship and the vulnerability of emotional intimacy create obstacles in their budding romance, leading to doubts and insecurities. This conflict delves into themes of trust and surrender as the rockstar navigates their reservations and learns to open up to love. Overcoming this internal conflict requires courage, authenticity, and a willingness to take emotional risks for a fulfilling partnership.

Chapter 14

Creative Differences & Personal Struggles

Writing a bestselling rockstar romance requires examining the complexities of creative differences and personal struggles between your story's characters to create a rich and engaging story for your readers. Imagine your rockstar protagonist, for example, Alex, is the lead guitarist of a famous band, and they are about to embark on a new album. However, tensions rise as Alex's creative vision clashes with the band's singer, Mark, leading to heated debates and conflicts over the musical direction. This struggle not only tests Alex's artistic integrity but also challenges their personal relationships within the band.

Draw your readers into Alex's emotional journey as they navigate the delicate balance between artistic expression and collaboration. Introduce a romantic interest for Alex, Lucy, who works as the band's manager and is caught in the middle of the creative differences. As Alex's relationship with Lucy blossoms, the pressure to choose between love and loyalty to the band intensifies, adding complexity to the story. Use this conflict to showcase Alex's internal struggle as they seek to fulfill their creative aspirations while maintaining harmony within the group, a journey filled with emotional turmoil.

To heighten the tension, introduce a rival band that threatens to overshadow Alex's group, sparking jealousy and competitiveness among the band members. As Alex grapples with feelings of inadequacy and self-doubt, delve into their past traumas and insecurities triggered by the looming threat of failure. Allow the unresolved conflicts from Alex's past to resurface, complicating their present decisions and adding depth to their character development. This psychological struggle will resonate with readers as they witness Alex's internal battle unfold on the page.

Explore the theme of sacrifice as Alex is forced to make tough choices between their desires and professional obligations. Perhaps Lucy's job is on the line due to the band's internal conflicts, placing Alex in a difficult position where they must choose between love and loyalty. By highlighting these moral dilemmas, you can create a sense of urgency and suspense that propels the story forward, captivating your audience and keeping them engaged. Allow Alex to confront their inner demons and face the consequences of their decisions, leading to growth and transformation as they navigate the rocky terrain of fame and ambition.

Introduce subplots that delve into the personal struggles of other band members, such as addiction, family issues, or mental health challenges, to showcase the interconnected nature of their relationships and the impact of unresolved conflicts on the group dynamic. By intertwining these individual narratives, you can create a web of tension and emotional depth that resonates with readers profoundly. As the characters grapple with their demons, they must also support their bandmates through their challenges, showcasing the strength of their bond amid adversity.

Highlight the role of communication and compromise in resolving conflicts among the characters, emphasizing the importance of open dialogue and understanding in overcoming differences. Allow Alex and their bandmates to engage in heartfelt conversations that address pent-up emotions and offer a path to reconciliation and growth. Through these meaningful interactions, you can showcase the power of empathy and vulnerability in fostering stronger relationships and building trust among the characters. By demonstrating the positive outcomes of effective communication, you can instill hope and optimism in your readers, inspiring them to navigate their conflicts with courage and compassion.

Explore the theme of redemption as Alex and the band navigate a series of setbacks and challenges that test their resilience and determination. Perhaps a scandal threatens to tarnish their reputation, forcing Alex to confront their past mistakes and seek forgiveness from those they have wronged. By delving into themes of forgiveness and redemption, you can offer a message of hope and healing that resonates with readers on a universal level, reminding them of the power of second chances and the importance of growth through adversity. Showcasing Alex's journey toward redemption can serve as a powerful narrative arc that captures the hearts of your audience and leaves a lasting impact.

Capture the emotional intensity of the conflicts and obstacles faced by your characters through vivid and evocative prose that immerses readers in the tumultuous world of rockstar romance. Use sensory details to paint a vivid picture of the band's struggles and triumphs, allowing readers to experience the highs and lows alongside the characters. Utilize descriptive language to evoke Alex and their bandmates' raw emotions and inner turmoil as they confront their demons and strive for redemption. By crafting immersive scenes that resonate with readers emotionally, you can create a compelling narrative that captivates and entertains, leaving a lasting impression long after they have turned the final page.

Incorporate moments of tension and conflict that drive the narrative forward, keeping readers on the edge of their seats as they eagerly anticipate the resolution of the characters' struggles. Introduce plot twists and surprises that challenge the characters' beliefs and motivations, forcing them to confront their fears and vulnerabilities head-on. By injecting these unexpected twists into the story, you can subvert expectations and keep your audience engaged, eager to discover how the characters will overcome their obstacles and emerge stronger on the other side. Embrace the unpredictability of the creative process and allow your characters to navigate the rocky terrain of conflict with courage and resilience, inspiring readers to embrace their own struggles with grace and determination.

Chapter 15

Mastering Emotional Resonance

In the tumultuous world of rockstar romances, conflicts, and obstacles are essential elements that drive the narrative forward, infusing the story with tension, drama, and emotional depth. A common conflict rockstars face is the clash between their desires and responsibilities to their band members or fans. For example, in 'Chord' by Chelsea Camaron and MJ Fields, the protagonist, Rock, struggles to balance his budding romance with band obligations, leading to internal conflicts and external pressures. This inner turmoil often results in a push-and-pull dynamic that readers find engaging and relatable, heightening the stakes for the characters involved.

Moreover, conflicts in rockstar romance often stem from the characters' past traumas or insecurities, shaping their present-day struggles and relationships. In Olivia Cunning's bestselling novel, 'Backstage Pass,' the band members carry emotional scars from their pasts, affecting their interactions and ability to trust and love fully. These deep-rooted issues create obstacles for the characters as they navigate their budding romances amidst internal turmoil, adding layers of complexity to the storytelling and character development.

Rockstars also frequently face external obstacles such as media scrutiny, paparazzi intrusion, and the pressure to maintain a public image. In L.J. Shen's romance novel, 'Midnight Blue,' the protagonist, Alex Winslow, grapples with the consequences of his rockstar lifestyle, including scandals and tabloid gossip threatening his burgeoning relationship with the heroine. These external challenges test the characters' resolve and force them to confront their vulnerabilities and insecurities in the unforgiving spotlight of fame.

Another prevalent conflict in rockstar romances involves juxtaposing the wild, hedonistic rockstar lifestyle with the need for stability and genuine connection. In 'Rocked' by Taryn Elliott and Cari Quinn, the protagonist, Tom, struggles to reconcile his partying ways with his growing feelings for the heroine, highlighting the tension between passion and responsibility. This internal conflict adds depth to the characters, underscoring their journey toward self-discovery and personal growth amidst the chaos of fame.

Furthermore, conflicts and obstacles in rockstar romances often revolve around misunderstandings, miscommunications, and external influences that threaten to derail the characters' relationships. In Kristen Callihan's novel Idol, the protagonists, Killian and Libby, face challenges stemming from misconceptions and past hurts that hinder their ability to trust and love wholeheartedly. These barriers to emotional intimacy and vulnerability create compelling obstacles that readers eagerly anticipate the characters overcoming as they strive for a happily ever after.

The dichotomy between the rockstar persona and the true self also serves as a significant source of conflict in many romance novels featuring musicians. In Kylie Scott's bestselling book, 'Play,' the heroine, Anne, grapples with reconciling the public image of the rockstar, Mal, with the vulnerable and complex man she comes to know behind the scenes. This internal conflict drives the story's emotional arc and adds layers of authenticity and depth to the characters' identities and relationships.

Moreover, conflicts in rockstar romances often arise from external influences such as family expectations, industry pressures, and rivalries within the music industry. In S.L. Scott's novel, 'The Resistance,' the protagonists, Lukas and Riss, face obstacles from external forces threatening to tear them apart and challenge their love. These external conflicts test the characters' resilience and commitment to each other, underscoring the power of love to triumph over outside obstacles.

Another common conflict in rockstar romance narratives is the tension between the characters' professional ambitions and personal desires, leading to dilemmas that require difficult choices and sacrifices. In Tracey Wolff's romance novel, 'Rock Me,' the heroine, Layla, must confront the challenges of maintaining her independence and pursuing her career goals while navigating a passionate romance with the rockstar, Christian. This conflict highlights the characters' internal struggles and the sacrifices they must make for love, underscoring the complexities of relationships in the limelight.

Conflicts and obstacles in rockstar romances often manifest in the form of addiction, self-destructive behavior, and emotional baggage that plague the characters and threaten their ability to form lasting connections. In J.T. Geissinger's novel, 'Wicked Beautiful,' the hero, Vicious, grapples with the demons of his past and addictive tendencies that endanger his relationship with the strong-willed heroine, Emilia. These internal struggles create barriers to intimacy and trust, propelling the characters toward self-discovery and healing as they confront their darkest impulses.

Additionally, conflicts in rockstar romances can arise from the characters' divergent lifestyles, values, or social backgrounds, creating tension that must be navigated to bridge the gap between them. In Jay Crownover's romance novel 'Rule,' the protagonists, Shaw and Rule, face obstacles stemming from their contrasting personalities and backgrounds, forcing them to confront their prejudices and misconceptions about each other. This clash of worlds adds complexity to their romance, highlighting the challenges of breaking down barriers and finding common ground in the face of adversity.

Moreover, conflicts in rockstar romances often emerge from the characters' resistance to love, stemming from past hurts, fears of vulnerability, or the belief that they are unworthy of happiness. In Samantha Towle's bestselling novel, 'The Storm,' the hero, Jack, grapples with emotional scars from his childhood, leading to a fear of intimacy and commitment that threatens his burgeoning relationship with the heroine, Tru. This internal conflict is a powerful catalyst for character growth and transformation as the characters confront their emotional barriers to love.

External conflicts in rockstar romances can also stem from external threats such as obsessive fans, stalkers, or rival bands, adding suspense and danger to the unfolding romance. In Karina Halle's novel, 'The Swedish Prince,' the protagonist, Maggie, encounters danger and intrigue as she navigates her romance with a rockstar prince, highlighting the risks and sacrifices of dating someone famous. These external turmoil and threats inject the narrative with suspense, propelling the characters toward a high-stakes resolution as they navigate the perils of fame and fortune.

In conclusion, conflicts and obstacles play a pivotal role in shaping the narrative dynamics of rockstar romances, adding layers of tension, emotional depth, and character development to the stories weaved. Whether from internal struggles, external pressures, or past traumas, these challenges propel the characters towards self-discovery, growth, and a profound connection with their counterparts. By navigating through adversity, confronting their fears, and overcoming obstacles, rockstar romances offer readers a compelling journey of love, passion, and transformation amidst the high-octane world of fame and music.

Chapter 16

Leaving Room for Potential Sequels or Spin-offs

Leaving room for potential sequels or spin-offs is a way of keeping your fans wanting more. By introducing secondary characters with intriguing backstories or unresolved plotlines, you can plant the seeds for future storylines. For example, in 'Reckless Hearts' by Heather Van Fleet, the band members all have unique personalities and histories that could be further explored in sequels. Creating loose ends or unresolved conflicts in the main story can also pave the way for future storylines. This can leave readers eager to see what happens next with these characters and their relationships.

Additionally, leaving room for sequels allows you to delve deeper into particular characters or subplots that may have been touched upon but not fully developed in the initial book. For instance, if a secondary character in a rockstar romance captures readers' interest, giving them their own story can be a way to satisfy that curiosity. This can also provide a fresh perspective on a bigger rockstar universe.

'Rocked by Love' by Christine Warren is a good example, as it features interconnected characters with the potential for their stories to be expanded upon.

Sequels or spin-offs can offer an opportunity to explore different themes or genres within the rockstar romance universe. You can focus on a different aspect of the music industry, introduce new conflicts, or change the setting to keep the stories engaging. By doing this, you cater to a wider audience and present a more diverse range of narratives. 'Shooting Star' by Arianne Richmonde, for instance, offers a spin-off series set in a different city with a new band, appealing to readers who enjoy rockstar romances but are looking for a fresh take on the genre.

Introducing unresolved mysteries, unanswered questions, or cliffhangers in the primary rockstar romance can create anticipation for potential sequels. Leaving some elements open-ended entices readers to come back for more and see how those loose threads are woven into future narratives. It builds a sense of ongoing narrative continuity and can deepen readers' emotional investment in the characters and their stories. 'Strings of the Heart' by Katie Ashley does this effectively, setting up scenarios and relationships that could be further explored in subsequent books.

Spin-offs can also offer a chance to delve into the lives of supporting characters who are not part of the main band but still play significant roles in the plot. Giving these characters their own spotlight expands the series' universe and enriches the storytelling. 'Loud is How I Love You' by Mercy Brown introduces characters beyond the main band, creating opportunities for spin-offs centered around their experiences and relationships.

Exploring sequels or spin-offs can deepen the world-building within the rockstar romance genre. By expanding on the existing setting, introducing new locations, or incorporating different elements, you create a more immersive reading experience for your audience. This can bring new life into the series and allow readers to see familiar characters in fresh contexts. 'Lost in Rewind' by Tali Alexander, for example, features sequels that take the characters on tours, further showcasing the rockstar lifestyle and the challenges that come with fame.

Sequels or spin-offs can also provide an avenue for revisiting beloved characters and giving them new challenges to overcome. By continuing their stories, you allow readers to witness how these characters evolve and navigate new obstacles. This can deepen the emotional connection between readers and the characters as they see familiar faces grow and change throughout the series. For instance, 'The Darkest Star' by Jennifer L. Armentrout follows the journey of secondary characters from the initial rockstar romance, giving them their own story arcs.

Moreover, sequels or spin-offs offer the opportunity to explore further the romantic relationships established in the main rockstar love story. By diving deeper into the dynamics between characters, you can showcase the evolution of their love story, introduce new conflicts, and provide fresh insights into their connection. This allows readers to witness the couple's journey beyond the initial book, experiencing the highs and lows of their relationship in more detail. 'The Silent Waters' by Brittainy C. Cherry extends the love story of secondary characters from the core romance, continuing their emotional journey and deepening their bond.

Using sequels or spin-offs can also be a way to showcase character maturation over a series. By exploring different aspects of the characters' lives and personalities in each installment, you give your readers a look at their arcs and how they change over time. This can create a more nuanced portrayal of the characters and their relationships, allowing readers to become fully immersed in their emotional evolution. 'Angel Falls' by Kristin Hannah demonstrates this approach by following characters through multiple sequels, showcasing their growth, challenges, and triumphs as they navigate the complexities of life.

Furthermore, sequels or spin-offs can introduce new conflicts, challenges, or adversaries to keep the story fresh and engaging. By bringing in new elements that test the characters differently, you can maintain reader interest and offer unexpected twists and turns in the narrative. This prevents the series from becoming stagnant and allows for continued excitement and suspense as the story progresses. 'Never Never' by Colleen Hoover and Tarryn Fisher introduces new obstacles in its sequels that challenge the characters' relationships and beliefs, adding multiple layers to the original storyline.

For readers who have grown attached to the world and characters of a rockstar romance, sequels or spin-offs can offer a sense of continuity and familiarity while also providing new adventures and developments. It allows fans to revisit their favorite settings, reminisce about beloved characters, and discover fresh storylines that expand the universe they've come to love. By balancing elements of the familiar with the excitement of the new, you can create a dynamic reading experience that satisfies existing fans while attracting new ones. 'Forever Rockers' by Terri Anne Browning, for example, builds on the established world of the rock band and its dynamics while introducing new conflicts and relationships to keep readers invested.

Meanwhile, you, as an author, are given the opportunity to experiment with different narrative styles, themes, and settings, further refining your craft and showcasing your versatility. This not only allows you to deliver a satisfying series where fans can revisit their favorite characters and immerse themselves in captivating storylines but also provides a platform to explore new horizons within the realm of rockstar romances, ultimately attaining a level of depth and complexity that satisfies both you and your readers.

Chapter 17

Importance of Having an Unique Writing Style & Tone

The significance of a unique writing style and tone cannot be overstated. The uniqueness of a writer's voice not only sets them apart but also creates a special bond with their readers, giving their work an unforgettable, distinctive quality. A distinct writing style and tone is like the author's signature on each page, giving the reader a sense of the author's personality, individuality, and creativity. It is what creates a distinct connection between you, the author, and your readers.

An author's unique writing style also aids in conveying the story's mood, atmosphere, and emotional undertone, bringing the narrative to life. It plays a crucial role in establishing the setting, character development, and relationship dynamics. This is important when crafting a rockstar romance series, where the rockstar lifestyle and the romantic relationships intertwine to create an engaging, immersive experience for readers.

Consider the impact of Suzanne Collins's writing style

on The 'Hunger Games.' Her distinctive voice and tone brilliantly capture the dystopian setting and character interactions, providing an emotional connection that pulls readers in. Similarly, Stephen King's distinctive narrative style has captivated readers for decades, setting him apart from other horror writers. His distinctive use of foreshadowing and suspense contributes significantly to his stories' chilling atmosphere and emotional impact.

Developing a unique writing style is not just a creative endeavor but a powerful tool that empowers you to create a distinctive voice within the rockstar romance genre, allowing you to stand out from other authors. This can be achieved by understanding your literary influences and what sets your writing apart from others. By leveraging this 'X-factor', you can establish a unique brand and make your work instantly recognisable.

Additionally, your unique writing style and tone contribute to the world-building of the rockstar romance series. How you describe scenery, portray characters, and depict interactions adds depth and realism to the narrative, immersing the reader in the world you've created.

From J.K. Rowling's enchanting descriptions in *Harry Potter*, which paint vivid imagery and set the wizarding world apart, to Nora Roberts's romantic and immersive style in her numerous series, each author's unique writing style leaves a lasting impression on the reader. This is particularly crucial in sequels or spin-offs, where familiar elements should be complemented by the author's distinct storytelling voice to ensure that the narrative feels 'authentic' and true to the series.

It is also important to note that a unique writing style can set a novel apart in the competitive publishing world. As more authors embrace genre-blending and unconventional narratives, distinctive writing styles can differentiate your work, making it memorable to publishers and readers alike. A unique writing style can give your work a unique angle, encouraging readers to pick up your book and continue through a series, thus retaining fan loyalty and expanding your reach.

However, it is essential to remember that a unique writing style should go hand in hand with readability and accessibility. While creativity is important, maintaining a balance between artistic expression and reader engagement is key. Your writing should be accessible and engaging, with a smooth flow of language that invites readers to immerse themselves in the story. This is where your narrative voice and tone play a critical role; they can add depth and personal touch while maintaining an entertaining and comprehensible narrative.

Your writing style and tone ultimately express your individuality as an artist, with immense potential to engage, captivate, and resonate with your readers. This distinctive 'voice' elevates your sales and builds your persona as a writer, communicator, and visualizer.

Furthermore, these forays can invite readers on a journey that transcends time. While some sequels or spin-offs continue the narrative in the present, others might explore the characters' past or peer into their future, offering fresh and captivating viewpoints on the relationship between the main characters. It can also provide an effective bridge for character arcs to evolve, adding deeper layers to their narratives. Just as 'Time is Ticking Away' by Rachelle Chase immerses readers in the dynamic time travel of rockstar romances, your series can likewise transport readers on a time-defying odyssey.

The intrigue of untold stories can often drive readers to seek more. Though not strictly sequels or spin-offs, prequels offer a compelling opportunity to delve further into a character's background, providing a richer understanding of their motivations and actions. For instance, 'From the Ashes' by Nora Roberts captivates readers by exploring vital events that shaped the lives and relationships of the main characters.

With each subsequent narrative, you can refine and evolve both the characters and the storyline. The characters can continue to grow and develop, their personalities and relationships deepening as they navigate the complexities of the world you've created. This allows readers to witness how their favorite characters evolve and adapt over time, building upon the groundwork laid in the initial work, much like 'With Every Breath' by Brittainy C. Cherry.

Early readers of your rockstar romance series will relish the chance to explore the nuances further through sequels or spin-offs. For instance, 'The Unseen' by Wendy Higgins offers readers a rare glimpse into the underbelly of the rockstar lifestyle, delving into characters' psyches, unraveling subplots, and peeling back layers of their intricate relationships. Following these characters' progression and love stories can further engage your audience, making each successive novel a fulfilling chapter in the series.

With every installment, you allow yourself to display your prowess in storytelling. This will enable you to experiment with narrative structures, character archetypes, and conflict mechanisms, demonstrating your versatility and imaginative prowess to your audience. In 'Unraveling Us' by Cynthia Harrison, the author effectively utilizes multi-perspective narratives, further exposing the characters' emotions and allowing readers to sink into the emotional depth.

Sequels and spin-offs offer an engaging extension into a world already familiar to your readers. They invite you, dear author, to experiment, explore unknown territories, and fully immerse yourself within the rockstar romance genre. They are the gateway to a creative universe, allowing you to sprinkle your magic unexpectedly. And through this artistic voyage, you continue to captivate and inspire your readers, encouraging them to dance to the rhythm of your lyrical storytelling.

www.ingramcontent.com/pod-product-compliance
Lightning Source LLC
Chambersburg PA
CBHW070507170726
48291CB00008B/2689